Creatures of the Night

Foxes
in the Dark

By Adeline Zubek

Gareth Stevens
Publishing

Please visit our website, www.garethstevens.com. For a free color catalog of all our high-quality books, call toll free 1-800-542-2595 or fax 1-877-542-2596.

Library of Congress Cataloging-in-Publication Data

Zubek, Adeline.
Foxes in the dark / Adeline Zubek.
    p. cm. — (Creatures of the night)
Includes bibliographical references and index.
ISBN 978-1-4339-6370-4 (pbk.)
ISBN 978-1-4339-6371-1 (6-pack)
ISBN 978-1-4339-6368-1 (library binding)
1. Foxes—Juvenile literature. 2. Nocturnal animals—Juvenile literature. I. Title.
QL737.C22Z82 2012
599.775—dc23

                                                  2011023332

First Edition

Published in 2013 by
Gareth Stevens Publishing
111 East 14th Street, Suite 349
New York, NY 10003

Copyright © 2013 Gareth Stevens Publishing

Designer: Daniel Hosek
Editor: Therese Shea

Photo credits: Cover, p. 1 Laurie Campbell/Stone/Getty Images; pp. 5, 20 Shutterstock.com; p. 7 Minden Pictures/Masterfile.com; p. 9 Nick Norman/National Geographic/Getty Images; p. 11 Radius Images/Getty Images; pp. 13, 15, 17, 19 Thinkstock.com; p. 21 iStockphoto.com.

Printed in the United States of America

CPSIA compliance information: Batch #CW12GS: For further information contact Gareth Stevens, New York, New York at 1-800-542-2595.

Contents

Boldface words appear in the glossary.

A Quick Look

If you look quickly at a fox, you might think it's a small dog. Foxes are in the same family as dogs, so they look much alike. But look again! A fox has a long, bushy tail. It also has a pointy **snout** and large ears.

Not Picky Eaters

Foxes live almost everywhere because they eat almost everything! They hunt small animals, such as mice, birds, worms, and bugs. They eat plants, too. Sometimes they even eat dead animals. In towns and cities, they eat pet food and people's trash.

Foxy Hunters

People use the word "foxy" to mean "clever" and "tricky." Foxes are foxy when they're looking for a meal. They mostly hunt at night. They have excellent senses of hearing and smell. These help them find food in the dark.

A fox can hear a mouse squeak from more than 100 feet (30 m) away! A fox may stand on its back feet to see better. It often can't see its **prey** unless the animal is moving.

Sometimes a fox waits by an animal's **burrow**. When its prey comes out, the fox jumps on it. The fox may dig a hole for its leftovers. It covers the hole with dirt. The fox comes back when it's hungry again.

13

Smelly and Alone

Most foxes like to be alone or with just one other fox. Each fox has a special smell it spreads across its land. When other foxes smell it, they know to stay away. Foxes also "talk" to each other by barking and growling.

Gray Foxes

The gray fox has grayish fur on its back. It has reddish, white, and black fur on other parts of its body. It's sometimes called a tree fox. It's the only fox that can climb trees! It climbs to escape enemies.

Arctic Foxes

Arctic foxes have white fur that blends in with the winter snow. In spring, arctic foxes **shed** their white fur and grow gray fur. Both colors help them hide from prey and enemies. Arctic foxes use their thick tail, called a brush, like a blanket.

19

Red Foxes

The red fox is the most common fox in the United States and Canada. Some red foxes have silver or black fur instead of red. Red foxes are good jumpers. Some can jump 7 feet (2 m) high!

The Fox Fact Box

Kind of Fox	Where It Lives
arctic fox	northern parts of Asia, Europe, and North America
gray fox	most of the United States, Mexico, and Central America; northern South America and southern Canada
red fox	most of Asia, Europe, and northern North America

Glossary

arctic: having to do with the area around the North Pole and other very cold northern places

burrow: a hole or tunnel dug as a living space by an animal

prey: an animal that is hunted by other animals for food

shed: to lose fur

snout: an animal's nose and mouth

For More Information

Books

Leach, Michael. *Fox.* New York, NY: PowerKids Press, 2009.

Person, Stephen. *Arctic Fox: Very Cool!* New York, NY: Bearport Publishing, 2009.

Websites

Arctic Fox

www.defenders.org/wildlife_and_habitat/wildlife/arctic_fox.php
Find out how this fox lives in its cold, snowy home.

Red Fox

animals.nationalgeographic.com/animals/mammals/red-fox/
Read more about what red foxes eat and the places where they can be found.

The Red Fox

dnr.wi.gov/org/caer/ce/eek/critter/mammal/redfox.htm
Find out how you can spot fox tracks or even a fox den.

23

Index

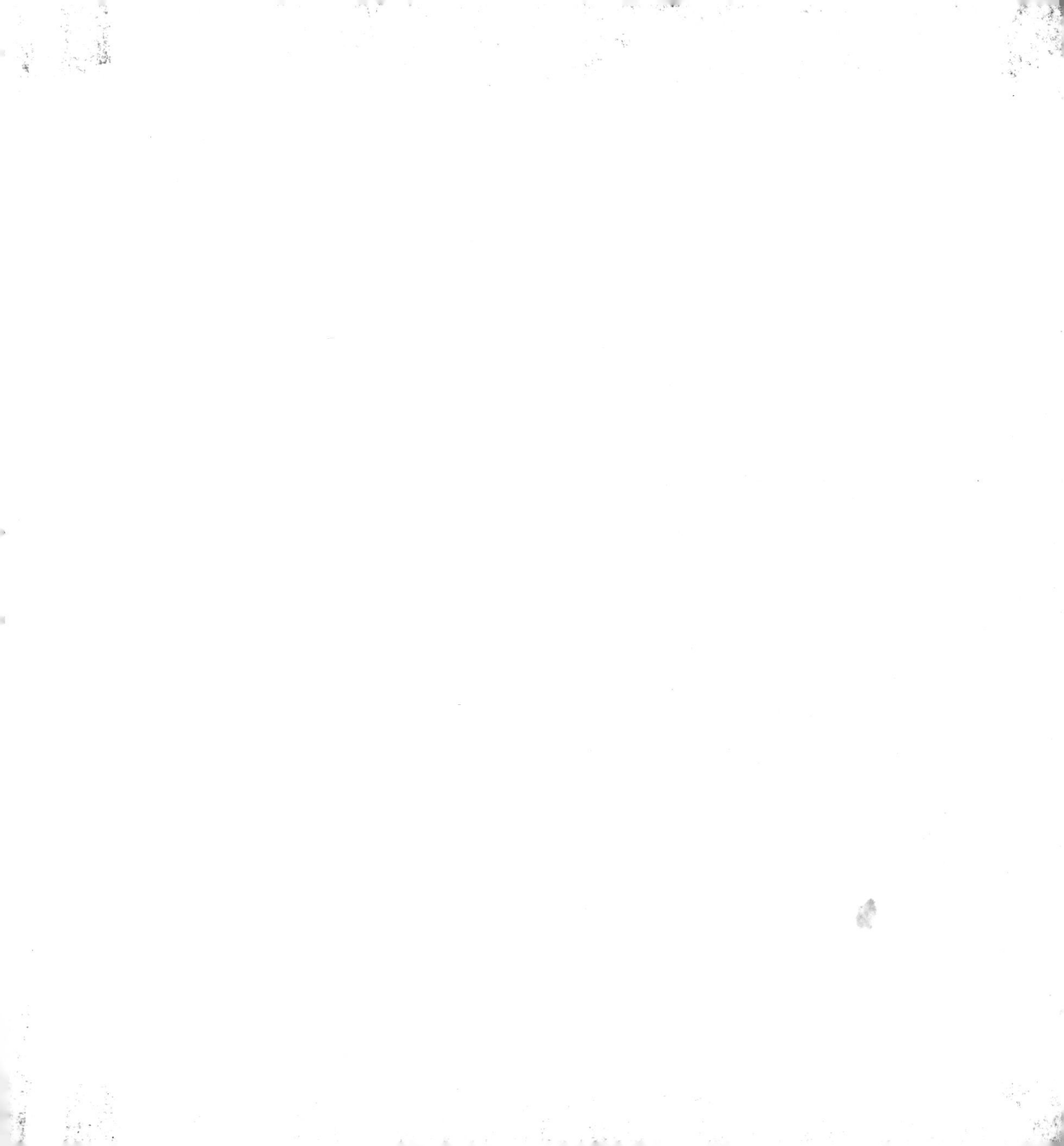